The Thing-in-a-Box

Diana Hendry and Sue Heap

Collins

This edition produced for The Book People Ltd
Hall Wood Avenue, Haydock
St Helens WA11 9UL

First published in Great Britain by
A & C Black (Publishers) Ltd 1992
First published by Collins in 1993
10 9 8 7 6 5

Collins is an imprint of HarperCollins*Publishers* Ltd,
77-85 Fulham Palace Road, London W6 8JB.

ISBN 0-00-763100-6

Printed and bound in Great Britain by
Omnia Books Limited, Glasgow

Chapter One

One morning, Mulligan's love,
Mrs Millie Dembo, came home with a

She had been away for four whole days and Mulligan had missed her dreadfully.

Now that Mrs Dembo was home again, Mulligan was delighted to see her. He was about to jump up and say so by licking her all over, but Mr Dembo said,

DOWN Mulligan! DOWN!

And Mrs Dembo, the love of
Mulligan's heart and tummy,
hardly gave him a glance,
let alone the welcoming
hug she usually gave
him even when she'd
just been down to
the corner shop
and back.

She wasn't interested in him.
She was only interested in
the Thing-in-a-Box.

Chapter Two

It was quite a special
sort of box. It was
made out of wicker and
it had handles and a
picture of a stork on
one side. Mr Dembo
carried it very carefully
up the stairs and
Mrs Dembo followed.
What was inside it
that was so precious,
wondered Mulligan.

Delicious marrow bones from the butcher's perhaps or a year's supply of sausages.

Mulligan bounded up the stairs after Mr and Mrs Dembo. They carried the Thing-in-a-Box, carefully, carefully, into the spare bedroom.

Mulligan had spent quite a lot of
time in the spare bedroom recently.
He had helped Mr Dembo to
re-paper it.

On Guard

He had kept guard
over Mrs Dembo
when she sat
in the rocking chair
in the afternoon
and had a little
snooze.

11

To his surprise the
Thing-in-a Box was
put inside
another box.

The second box was
too big to carry.

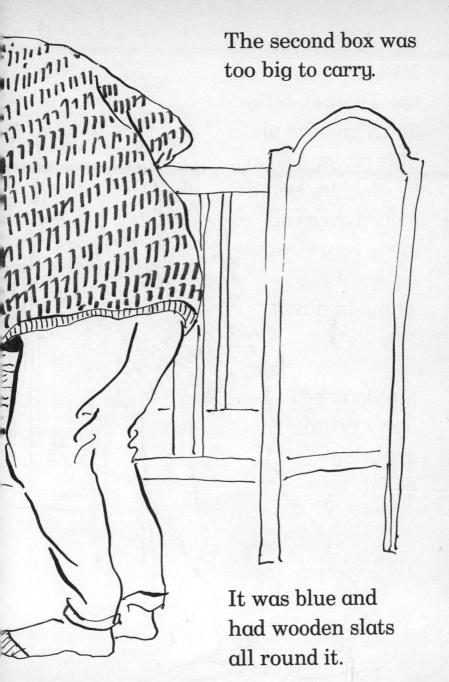

It was blue and
had wooden slats
all round it.

Carefully, carefully,
Mr Dembo lowered
the Thing-in-a-Box
down into the big
blue box and then
he and Mrs Dembo
leaned over and
made very strange
noises at the
Thing-in-a-Box.

Mulligan had
never heard
anything
like it.

Coochie Coochie Coochie Coo

That did it! Mulligan was outraged.
That was *his* question. It belonged
to him. Almost every day of his life
Mrs Dembo asked him that
question and Mulligan answered it
by waving his tail very high and
grandly (which meant, 'I am. I am
certainly a very beautiful boy!').

'Woof!' said Mulligan, by way
of a protest.

Mr Dembo turned round
and laughed.

And Mrs Dembo laughed too.

Mulligan was so angry he seized a
nearby teddy and tried to eat it.
At the same moment the
Thing-in-a-Box let out
a fearful noise.

Mulligan was so scared he
fled down the stairs.

He could hear Mr and Mrs Dembo
laughing again and the Thing-in-a-Box
still going WAH -
WAH - WAH - WAH
like a terrible alarm-clock
that no one could switch off.

WAH WAH WAH

Mulligan didn't think it was
anything to laugh at. He thought
it was the end of his happy world.

Mrs Millie Dembo had gone and fallen in love with a Thing-in-a-Box. She didn't want Mulligan any more. He was no longer her beautiful boy.

Mulligan crawled into his basket and tried, by curling up very small, to warm his lonely heart. How long was this Thing-in-a-Box staying? That's what he wanted to know.

Chapter Three

The next day was a very miserable one for Mulligan. No one gave him any attention. Mr Dembo took him for a short walk round the block but it was very slow and boring because they kept stopping to talk to neighbours.

Mrs Pennington from the top of the
street stopped to shake hands with
Mr Dembo.

Mrs Pennington laughed.

Mulligan looked at Mrs Pennington's nice plump little ankle and thought about taking a piece out of it.

He felt even more puzzled. How could anyone prefer a hairless Thing-in-a-Box that went Wah-Wah-Wah to him?

27

But clearly
Mrs Dembo did.
She only just
remembered to
give Mulligan
his dinner and
a very absent-
minded pat
to go with it.

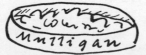

Lots of visitors came to say hello to the Thing-in-a-Box. There was

Grandpa

Uncle Dembo

Auntie Dembo

Grandma

There was a gaggle of little Dembo cousins.

Only last week Grandma Dembo
had brought Mulligan a wonderful
marrow bone and all the little
Dembos had made a great fuss of
him.

They had wanted to take him home.

'Oh no!' Mrs Dembo had said.

31

But now everyone ignored him.
They came with parcels and flowers
for the Thing-in-a-Box. They went
upstairs and they chirruped and
trilled and warbled over the
Thing-in-a-Box. And no one even
said 'hello' to Mulligan.

Mrs Millie Dembo was up and down
the stairs all day. Mulligan could
hear the rocking chair rocking.
He could hear Mrs Dembo singing.
But she wasn't singing to him.
He wasn't her beautiful boy
any more. She was singing to the
Thing-in-a-Box.

Mulligan didn't dare follow her
upstairs in case the Thing-in-a-Box
went Wah-Wah-Wah again.

So he stayed downstairs in front
of the fire, sulking and plotting.
Plotting how to get rid of the
Thing-in-a-Box.

37

Chapter Four

After supper was
usually the time
when Mulligan
and the Dembos
played games.

Mrs Dembo
would play
Shake paws
and
Tickle-my-tummy.

Mr Dembo would
toss a ball in
the garden
for him and
Mulligan would
race after it
trying not to
crash into the
flower-beds.

Sometimes they all played
Nothing-will-wake-me-up-except-a-chocolate-button. This was
Mulligan's favourite game.
He was very good at it.

But there were no games that
evening. After supper the Dembos
both fell fast asleep. The chocolate
buttons were there all right, just
sitting there, waiting, on the
little table beside the sleeping
Millie Dembo.

I'll start the game, thought
Mulligan and he used his nose to
rattle the packet.

Mrs Dembo
didn't stir.

Mr Dembo
didn't twitch.

Mulligan nudged the packet with
his nose until it dropped on the
floor. It made what seemed to him a
very loud chocolate button noise.

chocosplat

Not a peep from Mrs Dembo!

Not a poop from Mr Dembo!

Blow them both, thought Mulligan
and he ate all the chocolate buttons
and licked the packet clean.

Still the Dembos slept on.

Now's my chance, thought
Mulligan. While they're
asleep I can creep
upstairs and eat the
Thing-in-a-Box.
Or if I can't eat it,
I can chew it.

And if I can't chew it, I can shake it.

At the very least, I can find out
what it is.

Chapter Five

Mulligan climbed up the stairs on his quietest paws. The door of the spare room was half open. Mulligan slid round it. There was not a sound from the Thing-in-a-Box.

carefully carefully

Mulligan crept across the room to the big blue box.

44

He put his nose to the wooden slats
and sniffed at the Thing-in-a-Box.

It smelt very strange. It was not a
marrow bone smell. It was not a
box-of-sausages smell. If anything,
it was a rather Millie Dembo smell.

sniff

He was just having a final sniff
when the Thing-in-a-Box began
making odd noises. It wasn't Wah-
Wah-Wah this time. It was

sniffle snuffle snuffle.

Mulligan's curiosity got the better
of his fear.

Carefully,
carefully, and
lightly, lightly,
he leapt up so
that he was
standing with
his front paws
on top of the
blue box.

Then, just like the Dembos had
done earlier that day, he could look
down at the Thing-in-a-Box.

He saw a little bald head and a little bald nose and a little bald paw that was trying to find its mouth.

Just at that moment the
Thing-in-a-Box's alarm went off.

WAH WAH WAH
WAH WAH WAH
WAH it went!

But this time Mulligan wasn't
scared. He guessed what Wah-Wah-
Wah meant. It meant 'I'm hungry'.
So he sat down beside the
hairless puppy and
waited.

Mrs Dembo had been running up
and down stairs all day. She would
be sure to come at once when she
heard the alarm call.

But she didn't, nor did Mr Dembo.

WAH WAH went the Thing-in-a-Box.

I'd better go and get them, thought Mulligan.

Chapter Six

Mr and Mrs Dembo were asleep
together on the sofa. Their arms
and legs were all in a muddle.

Z Z Z

WAH - WAH went the
Thing-in-a-Box,
but rather faintly now.

Mulligan found a knee and gave it a
nudge, and then another nudge.

Nothing happened.

Mulligan found the hem of Mrs Dembo's dress and gave it a tug.

Still nothing happened . . .

Except that a small hole grew in Mrs Dembo's dress.

HOWL WOW

There was nothing else
for it. Mulligan sat
back on his haunches
and gave his very best

HOWL

It was the sort of
howl he gave when
they'd shut him out in the garden
and forgotten about him.

HOWL

It was the sort of howl he gave
when Mr Dembo accidentally
trod on his tail.

OW WOW HOWL

It was the sort of howl
that made the neighbours
put their fingers in their
ears. It was the sort of
howl you could hear
fifty miles away.

And like an echo, very faintly,
the Thing-in-a-Box called back

WOW WOW

WAH WAH WAH WAH WAH

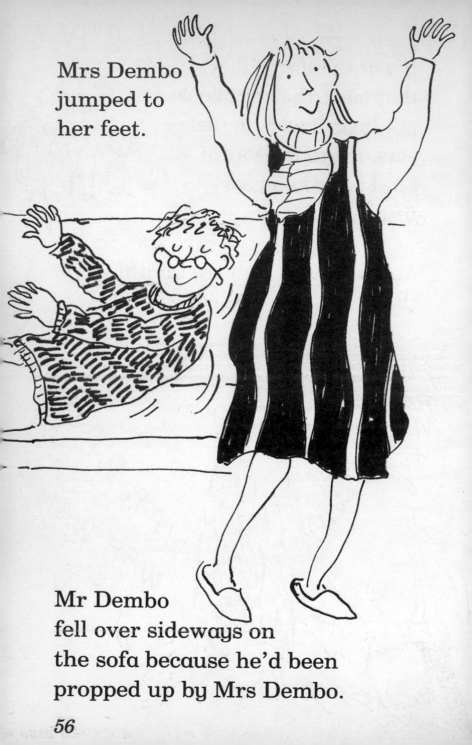

Mrs Dembo
jumped to
her feet.

Mr Dembo
fell over sideways on
the sofa because he'd been
propped up by Mrs Dembo.

cried Mrs Dembo, all of a quiver at such a noisy awakening.

57

Mr Dembo didn't answer.
He'd been having a very nice
dream. He snuggled down into
the sofa and tried to get back to it.

Mrs Dembo gave Mulligan a big hug. Mulligan's ears rose so high they almost came off.

He, Mulligan, had a new job to do.
Not only did he have to guard
Mrs Millie Dembo, the love of his
heart and his tummy, and take
Mr Dembo out for walks, but now
*he had a baby-in-a-box to look
after.*

Mulligan preened
and tried to look
modest all at once.
Carrying his tail
very high, he
followed Mrs Dembo
up the stairs to the
Thing-in-a-Box's
room.

Carefully, carefully, Mrs Dembo
leant over the big blue cot and
lifted the baby out of its carry-cot.
Then holding the baby in her
arms she sat down in the
rocking chair.

Oh, thought Mulligan, much surprised, so it doesn't stay in a box all the time. And he gave the baby's feet an experimental lick. The baby clenched its little toes. Mrs Dembo laughed.

'Let me introduce you,' she said.

She cuddled the baby in one arm
and stroked Mulligan with her
free hand. 'Who's a beautiful boy
then?' she asked.

And Mulligan knew she meant him.